Target: Earth

Target: Earth

BY E.T. RANDALL

Illustrations by Jackie Rogers

TROLL ASSOCIATES

Library of Congress Cataloging in Publication Data

Randall, E.T.
  Target: earth.

  (Alien adventures)
  Summary: Alone on a secluded lake, the reader encoun-
ters alien construction workers at work on an anti-gravity
building site. The reader's choices determine the outcome
of the plot.
  1. Plot-your-own stories. 2. Children's stories,
American. [1. Plot-your-own stories. 2. Science fiction.
3. Extraterrestrial beings—Fiction] I. Rogers,
Jacqueline, ill. II. Title. III. Series.
PZ7.R1564Tar   1985   [Fic]   84-2740
ISBN 0-8167-0326-4 (lib. bdg.)
ISBN 0-8167-0327-2 (pbk.)

10   9   8   7   6   5   4   3   2   1

Before You Begin
Your Alien Adventure...

Remember—this is an out-of-this-world book. Start on page 1 and keep reading till you come to a choice. After that, the story is up to you. As you make decisions, your adventure will take you from page to page.

Think carefully before you decide! Some choices will lead you to exciting, heroic, and happy endings. But watch out! Other choices can quickly lead to disaster.

Now you're ready to begin. Best of luck in your **Alien Adventure!**

Target: Earth

WHIZZZT! Your fishing line plops into the water behind your boat. Your vacation at Kinnicot National Park has been full of activity—hiking, camping, and fishing. If only you could catch something! You've been alone on this secluded lake since dawn without a nibble. After a few minutes, you reel in your line for another try.

Suddenly, a new sound drowns out the whiz of your reel. KA-POCK! KA-POCK!

"Machinery?" you wonder. "In the middle of a wilderness park?"

Now a tall metal antenna rises up from behind a nearby hill. You wonder what all those gadgets on it are for.

As the antenna keeps rising, you realize it is not resting on the ground. The whole structure is floating in midair! And the shoreline looks weird—as if all the sand had melted into glass. Is *this* why the fish aren't biting?

The fish don't seem so important anymore. The question now is, what's going on here?

If you're excited and curious about the mysterious antenna, rush ashore and turn to page 43.

If you decide you don't want to know about it, turn your boat around and head for page 73.

If you want to check out the antenna without being seen yourself, sneak ashore and turn to page 98.

2

"Hey!" you yell. "Get away from there! Those coyotes will kill you!"

The Skree's head turns. You gasp. The thing is wearing a helmet! Tiny lights flash on the helmet as the creature twitters and clacks at you. The Skree is speaking, and you understand it! "An intelligent creature!" says the Skree. "Tell me, Soft Being, how can I find safety?"

"Climb up a tree—that's how I got up here," you answer. "But hurry!"

"Climb one of these large plant-forms? I'm not sure that is possible for me." The Skree wraps its fore-limbs around a tree trunk, with no luck.

There is no time left. If only you had something to stop the coyotes. They'll tear that poor alien to pieces! Then you remember you're in an oak tree. Lots of acorns here!

You grab a handful of nuts and let out a bellow. "WHHAAAAAAHOOOOOOO!"

The noise halts the charging animals. You fling acorn after acorn at them. The acorns don't do much more than sting the coyotes, distracting them. Most of the pack turn and run in another direction.

Only one big brute remains. It glares wild-eyed as it snarls, preparing to leap on the helpless alien.

Turn to page 100.

The bark-faced alien sounds overconfident. On the other hand, the guards are all on his side. You bow your head and hope for the best.

You're led away to a holding pen—a small, open room cut into a tunnel wall. The pen doesn't need bars, though. Outside your cell stands a Skree warrior to make sure you don't go anywhere. You notice, however, there are small rusty spots on its shell.

Sitting in the semi-darkness, you lose all track of time. The raw-earth walls of your cell seem to press in on you. Then comes a clatter outside the holding pen. Your guard has keeled over in the tunnel. The rust spots have spread all over it.

"This may be my only chance!" you say to yourself, leaping to the entrance of your cell. Then you hesitate. Your guard no longer looks like a fierce warrior. It looks like a poor, sick slave, following orders.

Should you help the sick Skree guard? Turn to page 10.

Should you take your chance to escape? Turn to page 48.

4

Although the Vorn captain talks on, you hardly hear what he is saying. You're too busy running through the new knowledge that fills your brain.

This knowledge makes one thing clear. The captain is lying when he talks about coming in peace. Your new "memories" tell of planets being attacked and enslaved.

Acting like a polite young Earthling, you smile and nod at the captain's words. At last, the captain tires of talking to you. A robot guides you back to your cell.

But with your new "memories" you now know how the doors work. As your cell door slides open, your hand goes into your pocket. You pull out a couple of coins, and drop them into the tracks of the door. The robot doesn't notice. It leaves you alone in your cell.

You try to keep calm, but as soon as the door slides closed, you rush to it. Did your plan work?

"Please don't let it be locked," you whisper as you push with all your might. The door slides open!

You exit into the maze of passages. But your recently acquired "memories" make them familiar. You choose a safe route to the Communications Room. The room is empty.

Go to page 5.

You step up to a control panel. Your "memories" call it a Meson Communicator. Almost without thinking, your hands move to the controls. The crewman whose memories you had absorbed had served in the failed invasion of that distant planet. What was it called? Falabb.

You try to sort through the memories. The crewman had worked on a communicator like this, intercepting Falabb messages. It's a lucky break for you—and for Earth, too.

Thanks to the accident with the translating machine, you know the Falabb are enemies of the Vorn. Even better, the memories you got from that accident tell you how to get in touch with the Falabb. You even know the communications frequencies they use. You set the dials and punch in a message—a cosmic S.O.S.

Turn to page 115.

6

from page 116

As the creature scurries off, you head in the opposite direction. "I've had enough of these Skree-monsters," you say to yourself. "Now to get away."

You stay up in the trees, though, just in case you bump into another Skree. Luckily, you don't see any more.

Instead, you hear a piercing howl from the direction in which you're heading. You peer through the leaves to see a pack of coyotes, crazy with fear. "Probably bumped into one of those gray Skree down by the lake," you think.

The pack suddenly stops in its tracks, sniffing the air and snarling. Then you realize what they're scenting. Down below, you spot the small white Skree. It stands frozen, swiveling its head at the pack. The alien doesn't seem to sense the danger. The snarling coyotes come charging forward at the defenseless alien.

If you decide to shout a warning to the creature, turn to page 2.

If you decide to try stopping the coyotes, turn to page 27.

8

from page 35

You dash to the only cover available—the open supply dome. As you leap through the entrance, you pull out the power-rod Eeyipp gave you. "At least I'm not defenseless," you say to yourself. "I just wish I wasn't here."

Gu'ur from all over the camp are rushing to surround the dome. You twist the end of your rod, causing alien symbols to appear. Finally, you see the Gu'ur version of ZAP. Eeyipp told you this setting sends a blast bolt from the rod. Aiming outside, you fire. A big pile of sand turns to glass. None of the Gu'ur are hurt, but they're a bit more respectful toward you now.

"I'm hidden in the dome, and they're out in the open," you think. "They don't even seem eager to shoot at me. Wonder what they've got stored in here?"

More Gu'ur arrive. You snap a shot at them, and miss. One of the Gu'ur fires back. You jump behind the door.

The shot missed you. Unfortunately, the blast bolt hits something explosive stored inside the dome. You, the dome, and half the alien camp go up in a roar.

THE END

You hate to admit it, but the alien is right. You can't resist its will. Unless you think of something fast, you'll wind up kneeling before it, a slave.

"Use your head," you think, trying to keep your knees stiff. "No, not your head. How about what's *on* your head!" You grab your fishing hat, covered with hooks and fishing flies. Then you toss it in the alien's face.

It works! Bark-face is distracted for an instant. That gives you enough time to jump it and grab the helmet.

"NOOOOOOOO!" the alien cries as you yank the control helmet from its head. You send the helmet smashing to the floor.

As soon as that happens, the Skree guards start advancing on their former master. "NOOO!" the alien wails.

You'd like to see how this slave rebellion ends, but you have more important things to do—like getting out of this madhouse. Right now, the idea of fresh air and sunshine is all you want. And it's more than enough reward for saving Earth from the slave-masters.

THE END

"I can't just step over it," you tell yourself. You approach the stricken guard, wondering how you can help it.

The creature is barely alive. But its jeweled eyes glitter at you. As you look into them, you find yourself understanding. "Do not grieve, human," it seems to say. "For my kind, death is the only freedom."

It pauses for a second. "I and my race are beyond help. Soon we will be gone. But your race can be saved. Go now. Warn your people. There are secret ways to escape..." You listen carefully as the creature tells you the route. Then the whispering voice fades, and the brave Skree dies.

As you step around the still form, you realize the Skree's words are true. With proper warning, Earth can defeat the slave-masters. You set off to the secret tunnel full of purpose. You have a world to save.

THE END

The flying robot grazes your hair as you duck. It zooms on, to smash against the Supreme Intelligence's main housing. The 73,000-year-old plates crack and shatter while the robot bounces to the floor, spitting sparks.

"You have only won a few more moments of life, Earthling," the Supreme Intelligence booms. "My robot warriors will soon destroy you."

You try to keep your hands from quivering. There must be some way to stop this machine. That smashed-open casing reminds you of something you read about computers once....computers and what?

Magnets! They foul up computer memories! From your pocket you pull a large bar magnet. You use it to hold your fishhooks together.

"What are you doing?" the Supreme Intelligence roars as you rush to its broken casing. You hurl the magnet inside. "Stop!" Its voice goes shrill. Robot soldiers appear in the dome.

"AWWWWRRRRRRRR!" goes the computer. The dome goes dark. Robots collapse like puppets with their strings cut. The Supreme Intelligence has been erased. Its plans no longer compute.

You stare around the silent dome. Then you begin to laugh. "I don't believe it! I just saved the world!"

THE END

12

from page 94

"I'll take the kid to town!" one man says. "My car is nearest."

The annoyed pursuers lead you off to a campsite near the lake. "Yeah, go to the sheriff, Mort!" they mutter. Now you're scared.

But as Mort arrives at the camp, his wife is waiting. "What are you doing?" she asks.

"Taking this kid to the sheriff. Little troublemaker helped that alien escape. The one we saw last night."

"The one *you* saw last night," his wife says.

"Whatever. We're going to the sheriff." Mort is pushing you towards the car when four glowing spaceships appear overhead. Everyone stares in shock as a voice rings in their minds.

Let the young person go! Only you know it is the Skree commander.

"Says who?" Mort sneers.

A bolt of energy lances down at the car. The car melts like a candy bar left in the sun too long. Mort and his family run for their lives.

I say, the Skree commander answers. *And I'll be monitoring to make sure that my friend remains unharmed.* Frightened to death, Mort has no choice but to let you go.

Farewell, the commander whispers in your mind. *And thank you again.*

THE END

You freeze in the bushes, hoping you won't be seen. No such luck. The truck backs up till it's right beside you. Then a man in an orange windbreaker appears.

"I thought I saw a fishing hat in the leaves!" he says. "Just came back to see that you were okay." The alien child in your arms stirs. The hunter's eyes widen. "What the...?"

You explain things to the hunter, whose name is Burt May. "It's a long walk to a doctor," he says. "We'll drive!" You roar off in his truck.

Between the doctor's tests and the alien's brain-pictures, you find out what the problem is. "Carbon monoxide," the doctor says. "For us, it's a dangerous pollutant. But these aliens need it to breathe."

A brief time beside the truck's exhaust pipe revives the alien. Soon it sends new pictures to you—pictures of its own people.

You and May bring the alien child back to the forest, where you're greeted by adult aliens. One clasps the child in its arms. They are grateful. Then, in the adult alien's eyes, you see pictures of their camp by the lake. Aliens are choking, their machines blowing up. They board a flying saucer, which takes off.

"Leaving, huh?" you say. "Guess our air wasn't right for you."

The aliens nod. Minutes later, what you saw becomes reality. The alien saucer leaves Earth to take the colony to another planet.

THE END

Hazy light hits your eyes. You sit up slowly to find yourself in a laboratory.

Shaggy red aliens are at work all around you, putting samples into computers, examining readouts, making measurements and readings. They're dressed in neat smocks. As you stir, their dark-blue eyes watch you closely.

The alien scientists—that's what they must be—guide you off the examination table. You stand shakily as they lead you to a chair and let you sit down. The scientists stare at you—all except one. That scientist is looking at the chair. No, you realize, she's not looking at the chair. She's staring intently at something *leading* to the chair. A wire.

"Wait a minute!" you say. "I'm not sitting in any electric chair!" You leap up.

Turn to page 26.

You can't leave somebody in danger—not even an alien. Luckily for you, the robots have also turned around to rush back to the accident. They busily move away wrecked machinery. But they aren't touching the car, or the alien inside. They're just tidying up!

"These guys must be programmed to clean, not help," you realize. "I bet they don't know what to do." After they neaten things up, the robots stand around passively. The driver groans.

You dart between the robots to see the broken steel and glass ground-car. Inside is a small person— an alien child!

Reaching into the shattered car, you pick up the child. The robots immediately jump into action, clearing the last of the wreckage away. But they leave you alone.

The child is tiny and skinny. It looks like the kid has never had a good meal. As you move the child, it winces in pain.

Dressed in a silver jumpsuit, the alien is white as paper. No hair grows on the child's head, and it doesn't seem to have ears. But it does have beautiful eyes— dark and shining. There's something unusual about those eyes...

Go to page 17.

Suddenly, confused pictures run through your brain. You're flying. You lie in a heavily padded seat, looking at a screen—and the view is stars. You're in space! You blink, shaking your head.

These aren't *your* memories. Somehow, you're reading the alien kid's mind!

More visions appear. You see the alien's world. Everything is gray. The soil is like ash. All the buildings are falling apart. Nowhere do you see grass or trees.

"That's the world you left?" you say. "I can see why..." You're interrupted by a huge explosion. Another alien machine has blown up.

You see a collection of low domes nearby. Maybe you can find help there. Another explosion rocks the area. Maybe it would be safer to take this kid to an Earth doctor.

Will you take the alien child to the domes? Turn to page 22.

Will you try to get earthly help? Turn to page 49.

from page 91

"Let's try to trick him," you say. Moments later, you're walking up the hill, carrying a borrowed knapsack.

You don't get very far before Fred Samuels' voice growls, "What are you doing here, kid?"

"Just hiking," you say, trying to sound nonchalant. "I was coming up to see the sights from the tower. Sorry. I didn't think anyone would be there."

After a moment's hesitation, Samuels says, "All right, come on up."

Tensely, you start up the stairs. The signal for the big attack is when you reach the top platform.

As you reach the last flight of stairs, Samuels says, "You know, I thought that orange backpack looked familiar. Now that I see Willie McEvoy's initials on it, I'm sure." He aims his power-rod at you.

You'll never know how the pursuit ends. A flash of light and a ZZZZZTTTT! spell . . .

THE END

20

"The only way I'll survive is by obeying Mr. Beautiful," you tell yourself. You pick up a knapsack and demonstrate its function. Inside the pack is a radio. You explain that radios don't work this far underground. There's also some canned food. But before you can reach it, a Skree grabs the can and crunches it in its claws. The Skree decides, however, that it doesn't like cold stew.

The next thing in the pack is a dog whistle. You pause for a second. "How do I explain this?" you wonder.

What is that device, human? the Brain demands.

"It's, uh, used to call animals," you answer.

How?

You raise the whistle to your lips and let out a silent blast.

Then you stare in amazement as the Brain—and all the creatures in the Swarm—start shuddering.

Turn to page 93.

A robot marches into your cell and takes you to a room full of gray-armored aliens. They sit at a control panel.

A metal band is placed over your head. You see an identical band on the head of an alien in red armor. "This is a translator," the alien says. "Do you understand?"

You nod, and the alien goes on. "You are on a starship of the Vorn race. I am the captain."

"Lucky the old fool didn't burn out his brains with this junky translator," mutters another voice. You stare at the crewman who operates the translation machine. Then you understand—you're hearing the crewman's thoughts besides the captain's.

Apparently, the captain doesn't notice. "We Vorn come in peace," says the captain.

The crewman snickers. "Just like we came to Falabb. But they shot up our invasion fleet."

The captain's words fade as the translation machine throws off sparks. Something *is* wrong. Suddenly, you realize that you can understand what all the crew members are saying. You even know their names and the jobs they're doing.

"Wow," you think. "That crazy machine did more than translate the captain's words. Somehow, it gave me a whole set of alien memories."

Should you use your new knowledge to contact the enemies of these aliens? Turn to page 4.

Or should you try to figure a way to get off the spaceship? Turn to page 44.

22

from page 17

"Your own people should know how to take care of you," you say, running for the domes. Another piece of equipment blows up. You're shaking when you reach the entrance. Grown-up versions of the young alien are there, opening the heavy metal doors for you.

The adult aliens gather to welcome you, pointing excitedly at you and at the child. Then you're led through twisting corridors to the alien hospital.

An alien with wrinkled skin takes the child from your arms and lays it on a marble slab. An operating table?

The wrinkled alien motions you to another slab. You get on, then lie back. The slab is cool against your back. Then comes a prickling feeling. It's as if hundreds of little needles were jabbing up at you from the slab. You jump up. Tiny wires are stuck to your skin, leading to the stone slab! But the wrinkled alien gently pushes you back. Is it some sort of transfusion to help the alien child?

If you go along to help the little alien, turn to page 66.

If you want to get away from this room, turn to page 80.

from page 44

"What is that terrible thing?" asks the captain. His snakelike eyes are mere slits.

"You mean this?" you ask, pointing the starter at the trembling captain. "It's a personal protection device. Everyone on Earth has one."

"Everyone?" The captain's horror comes through the translation machine. He tears the band from his head and starts conferring with the others.

"This is it," you say to yourself. "Make or break time."

The captain shakily puts the translator back on his head. "Earthling, we will return you and your horrible device to your planet. We want nothing to do with a world that invents such savage weapons."

The crew brings the ship down for a landing. Soon, you're being bundled down a ramp that leads from the spaceship's hatch to the ground below—to Earth.

You look up, trying to hide a grin as the spaceship quickly lifts off. You may just have given your planet the most dangerous reputation in the galaxy. But you've certainly given these aliens second thoughts about invading it!

THE END

from page 116

Somehow, you feel you ought to keep an eye on this creature. You head through the branches after the small, white Skree.

The blast of a rifle shatters the silence. Bullets tear the leaves off a tree you just left.

A human voice comes from behind you. "Robbins, what the heck are you doin'?"

A nervous voice answers. "I heard something moving in the trees! Up there!"

"Stop actin' like a jerk, Robbins," another voice says. "A critter like this white thing don't have the build to go tree-climbin'."

A burst of laughter drowns out Robbins' cursing. You figure there are a dozen searchers in the group. They're coming closer. Soon you'll be able to see them.

Should you keep an eye on these searchers? Turn to page 71.

Should you try catching up to the white Skree? Turn to page 64.

Suddenly the friendly hands supporting your arms turn into grips of iron. You try to pull your arms away but you can't budge.

The scientists push you forward. Like it or not, you're going to sit in that chair attached to the wire. "Let go!" You twist and squirm, even aiming a kick at one of your captors.

More shaggy scientists close in. Among them is the female who gave you the silent warning. She leaps to grab you and suddenly goes flying back. Why? You know *you* didn't touch her. But she acted as if you'd kicked her.

The female alien falls against the advancing scientists, knocking them to the floor. She also sweeps the legs out from under one of the scientists holding your arms. With a howl of surprise, he drops. His grip breaks. Now one of your arms is free.

You tear loose from the other scientist and work your way through the confused tangle of arms and legs. Before you gleams one of the alien power-rods. You saw it used to lift girders and knock you out. Far beyond the glowing weapon, an open door promises freedom.

Should you grab the power-rod? Turn to page 78.

Should you run for the door? Turn to page 111.

from page 6

"I'm safe up here, but that Skree isn't!" You snatch at a good-sized branch. With a snap, it breaks off. Then you throw it as hard as you can. The branch catches a coyote on the rump. One loud "YIPE!" and he's running back the way he came.

"One down," you say, eagerly grabbing another branch. But in your excitement you reach too far. You slip from the tree bough. The leaves slap at your face as you frantically clutch for a new branch. Too late. It's . . .

THE END

"I'm not going to hang around here," you say to yourself. But you can't get out. The Vorn are blocking the door. You desperately check out the room. There's an air duct beside the screen, and it's just your size. You hop inside just as the Vorn burst through the door. With your heart in your mouth, you crawl away.

The air ducts are cramped and dirty, but nobody else is using them. You feel like you've been crawling a mile when you find a grille near a window. "I'll sneak a look outside," you decide. The Falabb arrow ships seem to be in a holding pattern.

"Come on! Attack!" you want to yell at them. An all-out attack may destroy the ship you're on, but it will save the Earth.

Instead of firing, the Falabb ships move into formation. They change course—for Earth! Hundreds of missiles flash from the arrow ships. They strike Earth's atmosphere with blinding flashes.

Your clever plan went wrong. The Falabb got your message, all right, but they didn't understand it. They thought you were warning them that the Vorn were building a new colony on Earth. Now they've just blasted your planet into cosmic dust. In all the universe, you are the only one who knows that the planet was once called Earth.

THE END

30

from page 53 / from page 72

After the sheriff hears your story, he makes several phone calls. One brings the doctor. The rest bring in about a dozen men. You stare as the sheriff unlocks the gun rack and starts handing out shotguns.

"Raise your right hands, boys. I'm swearing you in as a posse," says the sheriff.

"Posse?" you say.

"We have to check out your story. It sounds like trouble. Big trouble." The sheriff swears in the posse, and they set off for the lake.

Shortly afterward, you hear explosions coming from the park. You run outside to see a glowing spaceship streaking off into the sky. "A flying saucer!"

That's all you have time to say. A bright lance of light leaps from the saucer to the town. Everything glows with unbearable brilliance. Laser? Death ray? It makes no difference. You and the whole town disappear.

THE END

from page 58

You scramble into the suit. It's carefully designed for the round Falabb physique. On you, it looks like a limp balloon. But the Space Marines assure you it works perfectly.

You rush with the Marines to their assault craft. Soon, you're safely out in space. The spaceship behind you explodes with a soundless flare.

"We've destroyed the enemy fleet and the Vorn robot colony on your planet," the Marine leader says. "Now we'll return you to your home. Only you will know of the battle waged to save Earth."

And that's the way you intend to keep it. Who would believe such a wild tale, anyway?

THE END

from page 79

You turn to run from the mountain lion, only to find the shaggy alien. Terrified, you fall to your knees.

Lucky move. The mountain lion leaps, misses you, and lands in the alien's arms. The alien throws the surprised cat about twenty feet into the woods. The lion staggers off in shock.

The alien wears a harness full of gadgets on his chest. Now he touches a small box. "Do you understand me?" A flat computer-voice comes from the box.

"Y-y-yes," you say.

"Good. I am Hool," the alien says. "My people are called the Arfa. We come in peace to study your world. Several of your people are helping us. Come and see." You follow Hool.

As you reach the camp, some humans rush up. "Hool!" one man yells. "Fred Samuels has run off with a power-rod! We don't know what he's up to!"

The man turns to you. "Come on! The Arfa trusted us with those rods. It's up to us humans to stop Fred before he does something stupid."

Two aliens join Hool, who says, "We shall search also. If you wish, you may join us."

If you go with the humans, turn to page 91.

If you go with the aliens, turn to page 108.

What if Fred Samuels is telling the truth? Your rod-weapon is in your hand, set for STUN. You snap off three zaps. Hool and his companions tumble to the ground. You have thirty minutes before they regain consciousness.

Then you approach Samuels, rod ready. "Let's hear your proof," you demand.

Carefully, he pulls out one of the talking boxes. Sure enough, it tells of horrible plans. "Nuclear wastes will be dropped on the major cities," says a recorded voice. "All food supplies will be contaminated. Remaining population centers will be struck with plague. Study of native responses should show us how to deal with the disaster on Clov."

"See?" Samuels says. "They had a disaster on one of their planets, Clov. They were going to practice cleaning it up here."

For a second, you stand in silence. Then you switch your rod to LIFT. In a moment, the tree no longer pins Samuels to the ground.

"Come on," you say. "We've got to get that box to the Government. With that and these rods, they'll have to believe us." You and Samuels set off to warn the world.

THE END

from page 111

"They've probably found my boat," you say. "Maybe I'll try escaping up into the hills."

"Good choice," says Eeyipp. "No building is going on in that area. It should be easy for you to get away." She leads you through many empty corridors, until you reach an unused exit. "There are just two supply domes between this door and the hills. May Roo be with you."

Apparently, Roo isn't with you. No sooner do you step outside than one of the Gu'ur spots you. While the alien guard raises the alarm, you turn to the dome you just left. It's already sealed up. "Rats!" you mutter. "Now what?"

Ahead is one of the supply domes. The entrance is open. Beyond it stretches the face of a tall hill.

If you duck into the dome, turn to page 8.

If you run for the hill, turn to page 50.

from page 80

You watch the alien operate the blue ray. It uses a pair of joysticks something like the ones on a video game.

Summoning all your courage, you jump on the alien. It's a short fight. You tie up the alien, then grab the controls. On the screen, your boat still floats in the air. You make it slam into a robot. Then you aim the blue ray at a floating mast and tear it down.

In the corridor outside your room, you hear crashes and running feet. You keep wrecking whatever you see on the screen.

For the grand finale, you use the ray to tear off the top of a dome. Even as you succeed, you feel the joysticks heating up. Is this machine about to blow up, too? You decide to get out.

But when you open the door, the corridor is full of aliens. They look fighting-mad. Mental images hit you. You see yourself on the aliens' home world, wired up to several aliens. They're all feeding on your life-force. Space vampires!

You sink to the floor in horror. Before the vampires can get you, the ray machine explodes. For the next minute, Kinnicot Park is a confusion of explosions and falling walls.

Blasts throw you through a crack in the dome wall. The whole alien camp seems to be blowing up. You run for the forest, thankful to escape with your life.

THE END

from page 43

The robots close in around you, but you don't wait around to be captured. You pick a slow-moving robot and climb right up the front of it. Its metal arms are just a little late in grabbing for you. You've already leaped over its head.

Now you're outside the circle of robots. You run away as fast as you can. The robots grind off in pursuit, but you have a good lead on them.

You've almost reached the safety of the forest when a loud whistling sound makes you look back. The floating antenna with all the equipment on it is falling! It comes crashing to the earth—right on top of a floating ground-car.

No time to waste. You've got to get out of here! The robots are gaining every second! But from the wrecked car comes a cry of pain. You doubt that a robot could ever make that noise.

If you want to escape the robots, turn to page 104.

If you want to go back and aid the driver in the wreck, turn to page 16.

from page 92

You burst out of the underbrush and take off down the road. With any luck, you'll be around the bend before the truck returns.

You're not lucky. The truck roars into view, and there's nowhere you can hide. The truck coasts to a stop. The doors fly open.

The two riders aren't hunters. They're aliens, dressed in silver suits with glass helmets. They look like larger versions of the little child in your arms. And despite their alien faces, you can tell they're angry.

"I wasn't kidnapping him or anything," you try to explain. The aliens point crystal weapons at you. A flare of energy shoots out.

The next thing you know, you're lying all alone by the side of the road. You must have been lying there for a while—a couple of leaves have fallen on you.

The road is empty and silent. Was it all a dream? Something brushes against your hand. Caught on your belt buckle is a scrap of silvery cloth. Somehow, you know the alien child is all right. And something tells you that's the last you'll see of the aliens.

THE END

40

from page 75 / from page 114

Your companion grabs your arm, dragging you away from the destruction. "Up here, quick!"

Both of you stumble along the tunnel. Then you realize there's light in the distance. Sunlight!

Suddenly your muscles have new strength. You charge up the tunnel. You see other figures outlined against the light. They're humans, also escaping the cave-in. And just in time, too. As you emerge, the tunnel falls in on itself.

The whole hill that hides the nest is dissolving, settling into the earth. Mud comes boiling up. "Lake water must be all through the lower tunnels," your companion says happily. "Those bugs have just buried themselves."

"And their invasion is buried, too," another person says. "Now let's see about getting back to civilization." You all march off, leaving the scene of destruction behind you.

THE END

"Guess I'll try the right-hand side," you decide.

"I just came from up there," says the girl. "You'll find lots of food." She runs off down another tunnel.

But it's not food that you want—you want a way out of here. Creeping up the passage, you keep a wary eye out for guards. The tunnel opens into a wide gallery, with pits dug into the floor. Perhaps the pits are for food storage.

You're more interested in finding where the tunnel continues. Then you find out. The tunnel *doesn't* continue. The storage room has only one entrance—or exit.

That fact becomes quite important when you find a warrior Skree blocking the way out. Looks like the Skree decided to get whoever was stealing their food.

"Just my luck to get blamed for something somebody else is doing," you think. Those are your last thoughts because for you, this is . . .

THE END

42

from page 54

"But will this plague kill *all* the Skree?" you wonder. "Will it affect me? I'd better find a way out of here."

Perhaps you should have done less thinking and more listening. Something rams your shoulder. It's the powerful jaws of a Skree warrior—and this one's shell is glossy gray.

The warrior doesn't attack, though. It herds you through several tunnels. Soon the light gets brighter. You notice pieces of machinery, the first you've seen in this nest. You enter a large chamber—and see a human there.

No, it's not human, although it looks normal at first glance. This creature is taller and thinner, and its skin looks more like tree bark. It's dressed in a costume of constantly shifting colors. On its head is an elaborate glass helmet.

"Welcome, human," says the alien. "I speak your language well, you see."

"Are you a prisoner, too?" you ask.

The alien makes a weird sound. It is laughing! "No. I am their master. They are my slaves. But a plague is killing them off. That is why I've come to this planet. I need more slaves—and you are the first I've caught."

Should you pretend to accept this outrageous statement? Turn to page 3.

Should you defy the alien? Turn to page 82.

You head for the shore, but as you do, another antenna pops up. A pale-blue ray shoots from the antenna, right at your boat. All of a sudden, you're being pulled ashore. Your boat cuts through the water, zipping right onto the beach.

The wild ride ends with a jerk as the boat hits the sand. You're glad you're unharmed. But when you see your reception committee, your mouth goes dry.

They aren't people—unless people have started to be made of metal. Dozens of robots stand before you. Some have tracks, some have legs. Others stand on metal tendrils, while still another robot flies in the air.

You stand in your grounded boat as the robots begin to surround you. What do you do now?

If you want to convince the robots that you're friendly, turn to page 60.

If you want to run for it, turn to page 37.

44

from page 21

As the Vorn captain continues talking, you feel increasingly light-headed. It reminds you of the time Ms. Hartleberry tried out the deep-breathing exercises on your health class. You got dizzy. What did they call it? Hyperventilation? It meant there was too much oxygen in your system.

That gets you thinking. Maybe this alien atmosphere has more oxygen than Earth's. What could that mean? Your hand quietly goes for your pocket. You've got a campfire starter in there.

When you pull it out, it doesn't impress the Vorn. But when you flick it, a three-foot-long tongue of flame *whooshes* out. You were right! Fire needs oxygen to burn. The more oxygen, the bigger the fire.

The aliens shriek in terror at the flame. You realize fire must be a dreadful danger on their world. The captain, his staff, and the guards are all in confusion.

If you use the confusion to escape, turn to page 81.

If you decide to try using the aliens' fear of fire to get free, turn to page 24.

You realize these Vorn are different from the ship's evil captain. You can reason with them.

"I escaped from the spaceport, so the guards are searching for me," you explain. "If they see a crowd marching up, they'll just start shooting. But a small group could sneak in and do something to distract the guards..."

"While we get a starship!" the crowd yells.

Moments later, you're sneaking back into the spaceport—with six rebels to help you. Vorn soldiers are all over the place. You manage to reach the starships. But as you creep down the lanes between the ships, you blunder onto a squad of guards!

"Run for it!" you yell. Grabbing your arm, a young Vorn rebel pulls you into a small building.

"What is this place?" you ask.

"Fuel terminal for old-style rockets," answers the rebel Vorn, pointing at a maze of pipes.

"Rocket fuel," you say, an idea forming in your mind. "Get ready to run," you tell the Vorn as you work some controls. Thick rocket fuel begins pouring from the pipes. You pull out your campfire starter. As soon as you're a safe distance from the spreading pool, you create sparks.

VROOOOOOOMPF! The fuel bursts into flame.

Go to page 47.

"Now *that* should distract the guards," you say, running away with the young Vorn.

Your guess is right. The guards come running at the roar of flames. Their weapons are aimed at you. There's no way out!

But it's the soldiers who fall. Behind them surges the main group of rebels. They've broken into the spaceport! In moments they've seized a starship. "Come on!" says your young Vorn friend. "They'll be lifting off in a minute. You don't want to be left behind!"

You're safely aboard as the rebels leave their planet behind. They even give you a lift back to Earth.

"You have a pretty world. I can see why others want it," your young friend says. Even as he speaks, the ship zooms down to vaporize the secret Vorn robot colony in Kinnicot Park.

"Your planet is safe now. Invaders will think twice before they come back." The rebel Vorn turns to you. "Good luck, my friend."

"And good luck to you," you say. "I hope you find a good world to colonize."

"One we can colonize peacefully," he answers with an honest Vorn grin.

THE END

48

from page 3

You leap over the prostrate form of the guard. It doesn't even move. You rush down the tunnel to find what appears to be a wall of light ahead of you. "Well, light can't do much to stop me," you think, running on.

But as you pass through the light, you find resistance. It's as though the air has turned to jelly. You slow down, trying to push your way through. But you can't! To your horror, you find your arms and legs won't move. Even your eyes seem frozen, gazing straight ahead.

The bark-faced alien appears before you. "I sensed you might be planning something foolish," it says. "That is why I had the guard backed up by a stasis field. That is what holds you trapped."

The alien turns to its slaves. "Turn off the stasis field. The human cannot move. Carry the Earthling to the ship, then turn the stasis field back on, until we reach the home world. I shall have to perform some critical tests on this sample."

The Skree slaves carry away your unmoving form to a hidden spaceship. Soon you'll be going where no man has gone before. But this is one trip you're not looking forward to.

THE END

"I'd better get you to an Earth doctor," you tell the young alien. Even as you speak, one of the domes blows up in a ball of green flame.

You set off into the forest. A major road cuts through the park about a mile and a half away. You're sure you'll find some help there.

Carrying the alien child isn't easy. You're panting before you go a mile.

Then you realize the alien child is panting, too. You look into its eyes. Again, pictures flood your brain. You get a flash of the child standing under a gray globe—its home planet, you guess. The alien smiles.

Then you see the child standing under a globe of the Earth. The child gasps.

"Can't breathe our air?" you say. "I wish you'd told me that earlier. We'll just have to get to that road as fast as possible."

At last you reach the road. You're in luck—a car is approaching.

A new, insistent picture comes to your mind. You see yourself, with the alien in your arms, jumping into the underbrush to hide.

Should you follow the alien's advice and hide? Turn to page 92.

Should you stop the car? Turn to page 72.

50

"Can't let myself get trapped," you say, running for the hill. Gongs and howling alarms go off as you climb. You take a glance back.

It's lucky you stopped. A beam of light flashes past you. The beam misses, but gouges a huge hole into the side of the hill where you were climbing.

You scramble madly as rod-blasts score near-misses. Darting back and forth, you evade the beams of light. Finally you reach the top of the hill.

Trying to cut you off, the Gu'ur fire becomes more intense. The whole hillside starts to shudder. You throw yourself over the top. Cracks are forming in the rock. You've got to get to safety!

Running from the cracking face of the hill, you feel the rock giving way. A crevice opens at your feet, more than a yard wide. You stop short. The crevice gapes another couple of feet. You take a deep breath and leap.

As you land on the safe side of the rock, the entire hillside cracks loose. It rumbles down, burying the Gu'ur base. Hoping that Eeyipp got away safely, you lie where you are. You still clutch the rod-weapon—the only proof that remains of your strange adventure.

THE END

52

"I'll join the others," you say. But as you're led to the Pit, you begin to wonder about your choice. The prisoners are penned in a set of tunnels deep beneath the earth. The walls are damp. You wonder if you're under the lake.

Your guards don't tell you anything. They just push you into a room. It's full of humans.

"Another lucky customer," says a man with a big red beard. "I'm Charlie Conklin. You okay?"

You tell Conklin that you're unhurt.

"Good," he says with a grin. "Now could you please empty your pockets?"

"What?" you say.

"Look, we need to know if you have anything we can use," Conklin says. "Somehow, we've got to stop these bugs before they overrun the Earth. It hasn't been easy, but we're building a bomb."

"With what?" you ask.

"With whatever we have in our pockets," Conklin answers. "The bugs never bothered to search us. Members of the Swarm have no personal possessions. I suspect they don't understand that we actually own things. Anyway, with some butane torches and kerosene, we're almost there. You might just be able to help us."

Turn to page 114.

from page 64

"Run for it," you tell the Skree. "I'll try to get these people off your back."

As the Skree commander quietly circles back to the lake, you crash noisily through the bushes. "It's over here!" a voice behind you shouts.

For half an hour, you lead the searchers through the dense woods. At last, you're too tired to go on.

One of the searchers catches up to you. "How in..." he says. "Are you okay, kid?"

You don't look too well. Branches and thorns have ripped your clothing and scratched you pretty badly.

"Take it easy," the man smiles. "Hey, you guys! We've been chasing a kid!"

The others aren't too pleased to find this out. "Why was this kid leading us off the trail, and helping that monster escape?"

"Oh, take it easy, Robbins. The kid needs a doctor."

But Robbins won't take it easy. "Something's fishy. I say we take this kid to the local sheriff. He'll get to the bottom of it."

Rough hands grab you, pulling you back to the road and a waiting truck. Before you know it, you're at the sheriff's office. What will you say?

If you explain what went on, turn to page 30.

If you want to keep the Skree a secret, turn to page 101.

54

It's strange how your mind will dwell on small points as doom stares you in the face. You should be thinking of ways to escape this monster. But all you can notice is its shell. It's not shiny gray, like the other Skree you've seen. Huge spots like rust cover this warrior's shell. Not that it matters. Rust or not, this monster is about to kill you.

The warrior takes one step toward you, then falls to the floor. It lies there unmoving. Is it a trick? You watch breathlessly, but the Skree remains still. Finally, you step forward. The giant creature is dead.

Even as you watch, the rust spots grow. A foul odor fills the tunnel. "It's like some kind of plague," you say to yourself.

You leave the tunnel thinking furiously.

Should you hide and wait for the plague to wipe out the rest of the Skree? Turn to page 113.

Should you escape to tell the news of invasion? Turn to page 42.

from page 67

Ignoring the robot, you dash for the electrical cable. You get both hands on it and tug. It doesn't budge.

Meanwhile, the flying robot is circling around, acting like a bowling ball—with your head as the bowling pin. You only have one more chance. You grit your teeth and heave with all your might. The cable tears loose!

Lights go out all over the dome. The computers go dead. The robot plummets to the floor. You've killed the Supreme Intelligence. Earth has been saved.

You light up like a Christmas tree. But it's not all from triumph. This complex needed millions of volts to run. Now they go shooting through you—and that's

THE END

Your eyes scan the alien landscape. There must be hundreds of spaceships here, parked in neat rows. Just ahead of you is a fence. "A spaceport," you say to yourself. "But I don't think they want tourists. I'd better get away."

You start running for the fence, and find yourself gliding high through the air. This planet's gravity must be much weaker than Earth's. You can leap through the air even better than the astronauts on the Moon. The fence is no problem. You jump right over it. "I think I broke an Olympic record just then," you say.

But you land in the midst of a large group of Vorn. They're all armed and angry-looking.

"An alien!" cries one Vorn. And it means *you*. "Our leaders can find room for aliens like this on our starships, but not for *us!*"

"They've wrecked our planet," another Vorn says. "Now they board the starships—and leave us here to die!"

"We won't let them get away with it!" says a third. "We'll rebel! Seize a starship and leave!"

"WAIT A MINUTE!" you yell at the crowd. Amazed that you speak their language, they all grow quiet.

Will you suggest a mass attack on a starship? Turn to page 65.

Will you suggest a sneak attack instead? Turn to page 46.

58

Using your trusty *borpiz*-wrench and your borrowed alien knowledge, you smash the door controls so no one can open the door.

WHACK! SPFZTT! Sparks fly from the wrecked controls. Outside, Vorn crew members pound on the unmoving door.

You rush back to the Meson Communicator, broadcasting a new message to the Falabb. "If only they understand me," you hope.

The commotion outside increases. "This is it," you tell yourself. "They're breaking in."

A glaring energy-beam slices right through the door. Figures leap into the room. But these people aren't Vorn. They're short, roly-poly characters with round, pink faces. These must be the Falabb!

They may look childish, but they're all business, guarding the door with their strange weapons. One approaches you. It has special markings on its gold spacesuit, and seems to be in charge. "You must be the prisoner who led us here," the leader says. "We are Falabb Space Marines. Thank you for sending that important message."

The leader hands you a golden spacesuit. "We'll be leaving as soon as you put this on. Then this ship will be destroyed."

Turn to page 31.

from page 111

"Can you get me to the forest so I can reach my boat?" you ask.

Eeyipp leads you through empty corridors. You emerge from a side entrance of a dome, facing a wall of trees. You dash for the greenery.

All you want to do is get back to the lake and your boat. But you hear alarms and uproar behind you. Will you make it?

Branches and brambles whip at you as you run. You don't bother trying to hide your trail. Either you'll make it or you won't. Behind you now come clear noises of pursuit.

The woods end. You've made it to the beach! Dashing to your boat, you push it into the water. Then you jump aboard, gunning the motor.

You see shaggy red aliens on the shoreline, aiming their power-rods at you. Glaring beams of light flash. They miss you, raising clouds of steam as they strike the water.

Instantly, you steer into the steam. "Now let them find me," you think. Beams hiss blindly into the clouds. They just raise more steam.

By the time the air clears, you're well out of weapon-range. Soon, you'll be safe among the campers on the other side of the lake. You touch the power-rod in your pocket. Yes. You'll be safe to spread your words of warning.

THE END

60

You raise your hands to show they're empty. "Welcome, visitors from another world," you say. You've heard that line used lots of times in science-fiction movies. Maybe it will work now.

One of the robots also raises its hand. In its palm is a shining crystal.

"So far, so good," you tell yourself. What will the robot say?

It says nothing. The crystal gets brighter, though. Then a pink ray shoots from it, straight at you. As soon as the beam strikes you, you collapse to the ground. Darkness swallows you.

You wake up with a headache. You're lying on a plastic slab in a room with metal walls. The whole room quivers with energy, making your head throb.

Although you search hard, you find no trace of a door. You do find a flat glass screen with buttons underneath.

"Let's see what it does," you say, pressing a button. The screen flares brightly for a second, then shows a picture of a planet floating in space.

You recognize the planet. It's Earth. "I-I'm on a spaceship?" you gulp.

Turn to page 21.

from page 99

With the robots in pursuit, you run for the forest.

Good choice! Only the flying robot could have kept up with you here, but it went back to report to the Supreme Intelligence. The other robots crash into trees and break down.

Soon, only one robot keeps up the pursuit. It's some sort of earth-mover, with tank treads and huge, shovel-like hands. Nothing stops its pursuit.

You're running out of breath, but the robot has no such problem. It catches up as you stumble into marshy land. Leaning against the back of a wooden sign, you gasp for air.

A sign? You read the front of it: DANGER! QUICKSAND!

You form a desperate plan. Knocking down the sign, you dash to the far side of the clearing. All too soon, the robot arrives. You fall to the ground and the robot charges straight at you.

GLOOP! GLOOOPP! The robot starts sinking. Its treads churn desperately and its shovel hands dig wildly, but there's no escape. The quicksand sucks the robot down.

You stumble to your feet. There's much left to do. You've got to get back to your family—and spread the warning of robot invaders.

THE END

62

The stench of the Brain is making you sick. You no longer care what might happen to you. All you want to do is destroy the Brain. You're already in the air, leaping at this horrible creature.

Turn to page 97.

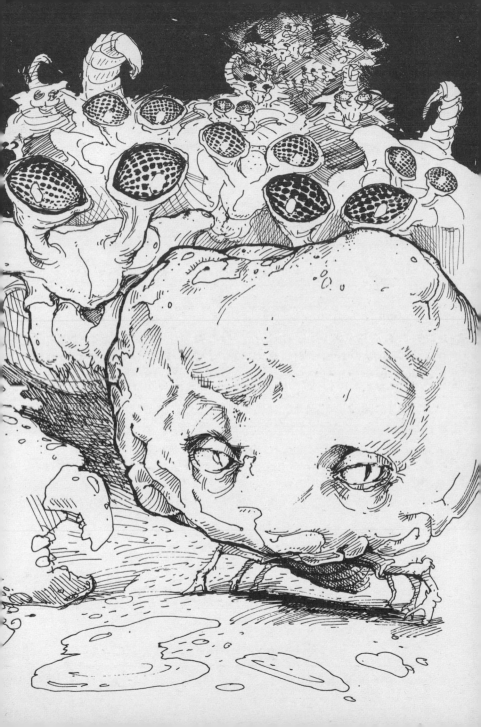

64

"Boy, is this creature in trouble," you think as you carefully make your way through the treetops. "Lost, and chased by a bunch of yahoos."

Are you a yahoo? asks a voice in your brain. You're so startled, you nearly fall off your branch.

I am sorry, the voice says. *Now I realize you use speech instead of the mind-link. And I see now you are not like the others who pursued me. I am a Skree, as you would call us. My ship malfunctioned last night...*

You remember the spectacular shooting star you saw last night by the lake. Some people at the campsite called it a UFO.

The other members of my expedition must surely be searching for me, the Skree says. *I ask if you can assist me in joining them. If so, I assure you we shall leave your planet immediately. We will cause no further trouble.*

"How can you promise that?" you wonder.

I am the commander of the expedition, the alien answers.

If you join the Skree commander in a race for safety, turn to page 94.

If you decide to distract the human pursuers, turn to page 53.

from page 57

"I'll help you get into the spaceport," you say. "Just stick together and show me the nearest entry gate!"

After they show you, it's child's play to leap over the fence and get to the gate controls. The Vorn rebels swarm into the port, making for the nearest starship. "Now we escape this world!" they shout.

All is going well, until you bump into the security squads searching for the escaped Earthling.

The mob surges at the black-armored Vorn soldiers, only to be met with a volley of disintegrator rays. "Run!" the rebels yell. "It's every Vorn for itself!" The mob dissolves as its surviving members run for their lives.

"Hold on!" you yell. "I've got a secret weapon!" You pull the campfire starter from your pocket. It terrified the Vorn before. Maybe you can do it again. Aiming at the Vorn soldiers, you shoot forth a tongue of flame.

The fire is terrifying, all right, but disintegrator rays are deadly. Before you even get into action, there's just a little crater where you used to be.

THE END

from page 22

You settle back on the marble slab. You'll do your best to help the injured alien kid.

The prickling continues on your shoulders, back, and neck. The hair rises on your arms. Your vision goes blurry.

You blink your eyes as the wrinkled alien looms over you. But now the alien's face isn't paper-white. It glows with an eerie blue, and its eyes are a color you have never seen before. "What?" you try to say. No words come out.

You bring your hand up to your head. Now your hand is blue, too. When you try to sit up, you're too weak to rise. But you can look across to the other marble slab. Now everything becomes clear. Sitting on the other slab is you—or rather, your body.

Your face gives you a sad look back as the wrinkled alien pats its hand.

Now J'Bork, you hear the old alien's mental communication, *you know we must gain Earthling bodies if we are to survive here.*

Now you understand. You're trapped in the alien's body. And it can't breathe Earth's air. Will you ever be able to leave the safety of this dome?

THE END

from page 103

You stand in awed silence at this revelation from the Supreme Intelligence. But your mind is racing. Is there any way to stop this gigantic revenge machine? You notice an armored cable leading to what seems to be the main computer bank. Is this a plug that could be pulled?

The Supreme Intelligence has continued speaking. "Of course, many races have resisted. I've lost many troops over the millenia. But I still have enough power to kill everything on Earth. You should be honored, Earthling. You shall be the first to die."

You turn in time to see the flying robot hurtling towards you. It looks like it wants to play chicken with your head. You glance from the cable to the robot, trying to decide what to do.

Should you get away from the robot? Turn to page 11.

Should you risk trying to pull the plug on the Supreme Intelligence? Turn to page 55.

68

from page 73

You dive for the bushes, then turn to see what the Skree is up to. The giant creature is moving slowly and methodically. It seems to be looking for something. You decide to move out of its search pattern.

Trying to crawl silently through the bushes is no fun. That's especially true when you hit some brambles. Finally, you reach the trees with only a few scratches.

You take one more look at the Skree. Its back is now towards you. You take the chance to shinny up a tree. "I'm no Tarzan," you think as you make your way from branch to branch. "But I'd rather be up a tree than on the ground with those things. I just hope they can't climb."

Turn to page 116.

The mountain lion keeps snarling at you. You try to remember anything you've heard about meeting wild animals. "Keep your eyes on it," you remember. "Try to stare it down. Show no fear."

Staring at the lion, you slowly start moving sideways. With luck, you'll circle around it. Then you'll dash for the woods. If the alien is still chasing you, *it* will find the lion.

"N-nice mountain lion," you say.

It might have been a good plan. But the staring routine doesn't work with *this* lion. You only seem to annoy it. Maybe mountain lions find it impolite to be stared at by their lunch. You'll never know. Because for you, it's . . .

THE END

from page 25

You stay hidden in the tree as the human searchers appear. They look like an assortment of hikers and campers. Many carry cameras. One carries a rifle. He grips it tightly and pokes it into all the shadows.

"Be careful where you point that thing, Robbins," one of the searchers says. "It might go off and kill a tree."

Robbins turns red. "You'll be glad I brought this when that monster turns on you!" he says.

From the sound of it, the searchers have heard this all day. "It didn't attack us last night when it appeared at the camping site. Why would it attack us now?" asks a man in a fishing hat.

"The only shooting we're going to do is with cameras, Robbins," a man dressed as a hiker says. "A clear picture of this creature will be worth a mint."

"Yeah, I can see the headlines," says another searcher. "'First Pictures of Kinnicot Creature! America's Loch Ness Monster!'"

Their talk is cut off by a loud cry. "SKREEE!"

From your vantage point in the tree, you can see what's going on. The white creature's luck has run out. It has blundered onto a bear!

Turn to page 87.

72

"Hiding won't help us," you say, standing in the middle of the road. A car comes around a curve, sees you, and stops.

"I'm Ned Harmon. Need help?" the driver asks. Then he sees what you have in your arms. "Where did *that* come from?"

You tell the whole story, then say, "We've got to find help."

Ned Harmon nods his head. "Let's head into town." You all get in the car and zoom off.

The alien's breathing becomes more labored. "How soon will we get to a doctor?" you ask.

"Doctor comes second. We've got to see the sheriff first," Harmon says.

"S-Sheriff?" you say.

"Sure." Harmon looks at you for a moment. "Look, kid, you did pretty well for yourself. But we're talking aliens from space here. Maybe invasion. I have to tell the sheriff. Then we'll get the doctor."

Too late, you realize things are out of your hands. And they've gone terribly wrong.

Turn to page 30.

This is no place to hang around. You turn your boat to speed away.

But you only go a few yards before you come to a jarring halt. The bow of the boat has struck something stretched under the water. It's a sticky filament of some kind, which reminds you of a spider's web. You have a terrible time, but when you finally get your boat loose, you decide to follow the strange filament to the shore.

In a few moments, you're standing on the beach, still following the filament. It stretches into a grove of trees. As you approach the grove, you sense movement among the trees. Suddenly a noise comes from the woods. "SKREE!"

"Skree?" you wonder. "What's that?"

Out of the shadows creeps your answer—a bizarre combination of insect and crab. Sunlight glints off its shiny gray shell, jeweled eyes—and fierce-looking claws. Those claws look big enough to cut through trees! You see underbrush nearby. You could hide from the Skree there. Or, you could run for your boat.

If you hide in the underbrush, turn to page 68.

If you run for the boat, turn to page 107.

from page 85

Should you believe a thief? Samuels is probably playing for time. His hands still strain to reach his rod-weapon.

"Please!" the trapped human cries. Hool and the other aliens aim their rods. You turn away.

The rods hiss loudly. When you turn around again, Samuels and the fallen tree have disappeared.

Hool shakes his head. "It saddens me that you had to hear what Fred Samuels said."

Now Hool and his friends are aiming their weapons at you. "Very sad. You see, everything Samuels said was true."

The last thing you hear is the HISSSSS... of their weapons.

THE END

"I'll go left," you decide. "At least I can hide behind all those sick Skree."

"And I'll come with you," the girl says. "If you've got a way out of here, I want to see it."

Running down the slope, you soon catch up with the tail-end of the plague parade. The sick Skree enter an area honeycombed with tunnels—and full of healthy Skree.

The appearance of the infected Skree causes a panic. Healthy Skree crush each other in the rush to get away. Others start digging escape tunnels. But these undermine the previously existing tunnels—tunnels now jammed with Skree.

In moments, the whole center of the nest is collapsing. You stare in horror as tons of earth cave in.

Turn to page 40.

from page 109

The Pit doesn't sound like a pleasant place to spend time. "I guess I'll work for you,' you say.

Excellent! the Brain replies. *Your first duty is to explain the uses of these artifacts.* Worker Skree appear, staggering under a huge mound of junk. *We acquired them when we captured the other humans.*

You wonder how many campers and fishers were kidnapped to collect so much equipment. It looks like the whole stock of a sporting-goods store, all piled in one lump. Even your boat is in there.

As the Skree put down the pile, a rifle clatters on the floor right in front of you.

Should you grab the rifle and turn it on the Brain? Turn to page 84.

Should you ignore the rifle and demonstrate how the things from the pile work? Turn to page 20.

78

from page 26

You grab the power-rod and leap to your feet. "All right!" you say. "Stay right where you are!"

The shaggy scientists slowly get to their feet. "No false moves now. Or I'll bounce you off the ceiling."

They start closing in again. "All right, now," you say. "You're asking for this!"

A little too late, you realize you don't know how to work the rod. There's no trigger. There are a couple of buttons, which you press frantically. But the scientists are upon you.

"Hey! Can't you guys take a joke?" you say as they take the rod from you and force you into the chair.

The good news is the chair isn't an electric chair. The bad news is that it's an automatic brainwasher. The shaggy aliens soon turn you into a loyal spy and supporter for their invasion of the Earth.

THE END

from page 98

Hoping you haven't been seen, you start crawling through the bushes. Was that a twig cracking behind you?

You stand up and take a backwards look. Among the leaves you see red fur.

That does it! You run for your life, tearing through the bushes. No time to get to the boat. Your only hope is to get to the forest and hide.

You gasp for breath as you run. Is the shaggy alien behind you? You can't take the time to look or listen. You dash through the trees, searching for a hiding place.

A snarl stops you dead in your tracks. "This is it," you think. "Cornered by the alien." But when you look up, you see a mountain lion baring its fangs at you. It looks hungry. This just isn't your day.

Your first instinct is to run away, but can you outrun this beast? Perhaps you can face it down. You've heard of people doing that with animals. But you can't take a lot of time thinking about it. The lion is about to spring.

If you decide to run back the way you came, turn to page 32.

If you decide to try staring down the mountain lion, turn to page 69.

You don't like the idea of wires poking into your body. Leaping from the slab, you pull free.

Aliens try to catch you as you head for the door. You dodge, and push your way through.

Your heart pounds in terror as you dash through the corridors, looking for somewhere to hide. You yank open the first door you find. But what you see in the room beyond puts all thoughts of hiding from your mind. Humans lie on stone slabs, attached to machinery. Beside them lie sick-looking aliens, also attached.

"They're using us to keep themselves alive— like vampires!" you realize. You burst from the room. Somehow, you've got to warn the world.

From behind you comes the noise of a search party. You duck into another room. This one is filled with machinery, run by an alien who peers at a view screen. You look over this alien's shoulder to see the lake shore. A blue ray is lifting your boat and bringing it toward the domes.

Turn to page 36.

from page 44

In the confusion, you run from the control room. Your Vorn "memories" guide you through the ship. "What I want is the Lander Station," you think. "I'll steal one of their flying saucers to get back to Earth."

No one sees you as you make your way through the corridors. At last, you make it to the Lander Station. You jab your fingers at a button, and the door slides aside. It takes only a second to climb inside a saucer and open the station's outer hatch.

You blink in surprise. Instead of the blackness of space, you see sand! "Could I have blown it?" you wonder. "Did we never leave the Earth?"

There's not a second to lose. The control room will detect that this hatch has opened. You dart out of the saucer and leap for the opening, tumbling into the sand. You're free!

But even as you get to your feet, you realize something is wrong. The sand looks purplish. The air smells funny. A red and a blue sun both shine down on you from the sky.

At last it's clear. The ship *did* lift off. You're on another world.

Turn to page 57.

from page 42

This bark-faced alien must be out of its mind! "You think you can make *me* a slave?" you say.

"Why not?" the alien says. "My people have been doing it for centuries with our insect slaves."

The alien touches its ornate helmet. "We also have the technology to do the job." It makes an adjustment to one of the decorations.

All of a sudden, you have an overwhelming urge to fall to your knees.

"You see," the alien says, "the control helmet turns my thoughts into irresistible commands. Soon you will have no will to fight me."

Turn to page 9.

from page 76

You grab for the rifle at your feet. "If I can get one shot at the Brain!" you think.

Even as you turn, dozens of Skree leap on you. The rifle is wrenched from your hands.

Treacherous human! thunders the Brain. *You have failed the test of loyalty. That Earth-weapon was left among the artifacts as a test. Its ammunition has been neutralized.*

Glaring at you, the Brain passes sentence. *The Swarm has no use for servants who disobey. Let this human perish with the others in the Pit.*

Your captors now seize your arms and legs. You struggle wildly, but there's no escape. The Skree guards pick you up and carry you to a huge hole in the floor. You hadn't noticed that part of the chamber before.

You struggle harder, but it's no use. The Skree hurl you over the brink. You tumble down, down, down—into the foul Pit.

THE END

from page 108

You and the three Arfa come up to Fred Samuels. His stolen rod-weapon has flown from his hands. He struggles to get at it. Then he sees you.

"You're a human. Help me!" he shouts. "These aliens aren't as friendly as they seem. They're not here just to study us. I found one of their talking boxes back at the camp. It was full of plans. Plans for *experiments*."

Samuels voice shakes. "The Arfa have messed up their worlds. Now they have to find a safe way to clean them up. So they're going to cause ecological disasters here on Earth. Then they can see how *we* deal with them. Millions of people will die. We've got to stop them!"

Samuels looks pleadingly into your eyes. "I have proof. I took their box with me." Is he telling the truth? He seems downright desperate.

If you think Samuels is telling the truth, turn to page 34.

If you think he's only playing for time, turn to page 74.

from page 114

The tunnels amplified the sound of the explosion. You can hardly hear your own voice as you speak after the blast.

"I'll stay on my own." You suspect crowds of running humans might get the attention of the Swarm.

"Okay, kid—good luck!" Conklin runs off down a tunnel. The others have already disappeared.

You pick a tunnel and start trotting along, your ears still ringing from the blast. When your ears clear, you hear the sound of rushing water. The humans have succeeded! They'll flood out the Swarm's nest!

You push yourself a little harder. It wouldn't do to get caught in the flood yourself. But you figure the next turn will start heading up.

Instead, the passage is a dead end. And as you turn from the blank wall, you see a new wall. This one's made of water, and it's rushing at you.

THE END

from page 71

"Hold it!" you shout to the searchers.

Robbins nearly blows you out of the tree with his rifle. "What is this?" he blusters.

"The creature you're following—it's in trouble," you explain as you scramble down the tree.

The angry bear towers over the white creature, which turns its jeweled eyes to you. *Please . . .* the word seems to whisper in your mind. Did the other people hear it, too?

"It talks!" you yell. "Didn't you hear?"

Robbins aims his gun. He looks like he can't decide which creature to shoot first—the Skree or the bear. "That creature talked to us!" you say.

Robbins makes up his mind. He fires three warning shots over the bear's head, which send it running off. "The white thing...talked," Robbins says faintly.

All of you lead the alien back to the lake. Along the way, you meet more Skree—attracted by the gunshots, you suppose. Soon, you're back where your adventure began. But now you see a huge glowing disk floating just above the ground.

I — Captain . . . the mind-voice whispers. *Lost — you help — thank you . . .* The aliens disappear into the glow. Then the disk streaks into the sky.

"Beautiful," Robbins says after it's all over.

"And you know what?" one of the hikers suddenly says. "None of us thought to take pictures!"

THE END

88

from page 107

"I can't let this big bug march me off to prison," you tell yourself. "It's now or never."

You race ahead of your captor, and turn down the first side-tunnel you find. The Skree starts scuttling after you, but you manage to lose it after a few turns. You dash madly, bumping into tunnel walls. To your surprise, the deeper underground you go, the easier it is to see. Something smeared on the wall emits a ghostly glow.

At last you slow down. Out of breath, you can't run another step. "Just as well that overgrown cockroach couldn't run," you think, turning a corner. You freeze.

Standing before you is a hulking Skree warrior. Its claws are out, blocking the whole tunnel. And its deadly stinger scrapes the tunnel ceiling.

Turn to page 54.

It takes all you've got, but you swing the door open. The sick Skree come pouring out.

"Hope you infect all the rest," you whisper. You trail behind the parade of former prisoners, hoping to find a way out of this nest.

Soon you come to a fork in the tunnel. The right-hand passageway slopes upward. The left-hand tunnel slants downward. All the sick Skree take the left-hand tunnel. Maybe you should keep following them. But what if the right-hand path is an escape route? You stop, puzzled.

A figure scampers down from the right-hand path. It's a human being—a girl. "Are you okay?" you whisper to her.

"I've looked better," she answers with a grin. "Playing hide-and-seek with the bugs gets messy. I've been down here for a couple of days now."

"I just escaped," you say.

"Here's some good advice. Watch out for the bugs. They're always hungry. And they'll eat anything—even us. I think that's why they came here." She shudders for a moment, then points at the right-hand tunnel. "This tunnel I came down leads to food—and guards. It's dangerous. But the left one is dangerous, too. It goes to Bugtown, where most of them live."

If you go to the left, turn to page 75.

If you go to the right, turn to page 41.

from page 32

The group of humans is led by a hiker named Al Fosca. "The Arfa are great trackers, but we know where Fred is heading," he says. "There's a fire watchtower a couple of miles away."

Marching through the forest, you talk with Fosca. He met the Arfa two weeks ago and has been working with them ever since. "Their home planet was nearly destroyed by war. Only a few Arfa remain. They observe other races, studying how to rebuild their society."

"Why did Samuels steal the rod?" you ask.

"Old Fred is ambitious," Fosca replies. "He looks on his power-rod as a magic wand, something to make him king of the world. Better be quiet," he suddenly whispers. "We're getting close to the fire tower."

Before you stretches an empty hillside, with the ranger station at the crest. The station looks empty. Then you see a head in a window.

"We could rush him," Fosca says. "But he'd get a lot of us on the hillside." He turns to you. "Or . . . Fred's never seen you before. You might be able to talk your way up there—and jump him when we make our move. It's your choice."

If you rush the station, turn to page 96.

If you try talking your way in, turn to page 18.

"I hope you have a good reason for this," you say, leaping into the bushes. No sooner are you hidden than a four-wheel-drive truck roars by. You get a glimpse of rifles stacked by the windows. And was that a deer tied to the front fender?

"Hunters!" you shudder. "Maybe you had the right idea after all. I'd hate for us to wind up as a hunting accident."

The alien's breathing has grown worse. It's just making shallow gasps. You don't need to be a doctor to guess it needs help right away.

"There's a ranger station down the road a bit," you say. "They should be able to help you."

Before you get onto the road, though, you hear the roar of a returning engine. The hunters are coming back!

If you decide to stay hidden, turn to page 13.

If you decide to run for the station, turn to page 39.

from page 20

You've learned something about the Skree—they can't stand ultrasonic vibrations!

You take a deep breath and give them another dose of the dog whistle. It makes their shuddering worse. The Brain's six legs move spastically. None of the Skree can walk or attack. You suspect they can't even think. As long as your breath holds out, you're safe.

Another soundless blast, and the smaller workers start thudding to the floor. After a few more tweets, even the huge warriors shudder their last. The Brain's evil eyes stare at you with hatred. But soon even they dull over in death.

You keep blowing the whistle until you can blow no more. The chamber is absolutely still. It looks like a battlefield, and you are the victor.

You breathe a sigh of relief. The menace of the Skree is no more. "Serves them right," you say. "What a bunch of crabs they were!"

THE END

94

from page 64

Your mind-link with the Skree helps it avoid the pursuers easily. From your position in the tree, you scout an easy route around the humans for the Skree.

When the danger is past, you climb down the tree. Then the two of you race back to the hill where you first saw the mysterious mast rise. Finally, the pursuers catch on to your trick. But they're far behind you now.

As you climb the hill, you're met by a search party of Skree. A glowing globe of light rises from a hollow behind the hill. It's the Skree spaceship. In moments, the aliens dismantle their equipment. Then they board the ship. *Farewell, and thank you,* says the Skree commander. The ship lifts off safely.

You're still waving good-bye when a dozen hands grab you. You had forgotten about the human pursuers! "Let's take the kid to town," one man says. "We'll find out what was going on with that alien monster."

Turn to page 12.

"I think Samuels would smell a rat if I came walking up," you say.

"We'll all go together," Fosca says. Your companions pull out their power-rods. "Ready? Let's go!"

You charge up the hill. Samuels starts firing his rod, and people fall. "We're lucky!" Fosca yells. "He's only got the rod set on stun!"

Still, watching all those people fall is scary. More drop as you climb the stairs. Only four of you make it to the top platform. You hurl yourself at Samuels' knees. As he falls, his rod smashes into a table and snaps in two.

"All right, you caught me," Samuels snarls. "But the secret's out about your precious Arfa. I called the forest rangers on the radio here. They'll be here any minute."

"You did *what?*" Fosca explodes. "We gave our word to keep the Arfa's presence a secret."

Samuels gives him a nasty smile. "Well, the rangers will have a lot of questions. And I'll have a lot of answers."

"I have an idea," you say. "But first we'll need the rods to move all the stunned people."

By the time the rangers arrive, the stunned members of the search party are hidden in the forest. But Samuels greets them with, "Have I got a story to tell you!"

Turn to page 110.

WHAT? the Brain's thoughts crackle in your mind. But you're on top of it. A stinger whizzes behind you, but misses.

The Brain tries to escape. Its oversize head wobbles worse than ever. Suddenly, it loses its balance. With a splintering crash, the creature falls over.

A couple of shudders, a twitch or two, and the creature is still. You didn't even touch it. It just overstrained its puny body. The Brain is dead.

You stand frozen, hands upraised. At any second, you expect vengeful stingers to strike your back. Moments pass. Nothing happens.

Finally, you force yourself to turn back to the chamber. The Skree rush back and forth aimlessly, bumping into each other. They're all carrying huge eggs—thousands of them. But they're completely lost without their Brain.

"So that's why they're here," you realize. "They meant to turn Earth into a hatching ground, and human beings into baby food, I bet."

Now, however, the eggs are being destroyed and eaten by the mindless Skree. You suspect the stupid beasts won't survive very long, anyway. But right now, you don't care. You rush away, glad to have saved Earth from destruction.

THE END

from page 1

You row quietly past the strange construction site, then steer the boat ashore.

"Next stop, the top of that hill," you say to yourself. "The bushes up there should hide me. And I'll get a good look at what's going on."

Sure enough, you have a clear view. And what you see below is more than an anti-gravity building site. You've found the strangest construction workers in the world.

Erecting the domes, masts, and walls are many strange, tall creatures. They leap about their work with greyhound speed and catlike agility. But they're like no people or animals you've ever seen. For one thing, they're covered all over with red, shaggy fur.

You watch with interest as one alien worker points a glowing rod at some girders. Like magic, the heavy materials float into the air. You gasp. The alien's tufted ears twitch. Then its head—and the glowing power-rod—turn in your direction.

Should you lie still and hope you're not noticed? Turn to page 106.

Should you crawl away through the bushes? Turn to page 79.

from page 104

"These robots are all falling apart!" you think delightedly. But there are dozens of them and only one of you.

The robots start closing in on you again. But the flying robot that had hovered overhead leaves the circle around you. "Must report to Supreme Intelligence . . ." it squawks.

You dart through the gap in the wall of robots, and run like mad. The robots begin to grind after you in pursuit, but you hesitate. You know you should get out of there. On the other hand, you're curious about this "Supreme Intelligence."

If you decide to keep running, turn to page 61.

If you want to double back and check out the Supreme Intelligence, turn to page 103.

from page 2

You take a deep breath, then scramble down the tree. You're not strong enough to stop the maddened coyote. But maybe you can distract it. And maybe the white Skree can get away while the coyote chases you back up the tree.

Well, part of your plan works. The coyote turns aside in mid-leap to go after you. Unfortunately, the heel of your shoe picks this time to get caught in some roots. Down you go, with the coyote pouncing on you.

A flare of energy blinds you. When you can see again, a little puff of smoke floats where the coyote used to be.

The white Skree is still there, only now it has company. A large gray-plated Skree looms over you. This one has huge, menacing claws *plus* a stinger like a scorpion. It's also about to attack you.

"Stop, lieutenant," says the white Skree. "This Earthling has saved my life."

The huge warrior bows and obeys. "Yes, my queen," it twitters.

You haven't saved an it. You've saved a she— the Queen of the Skree Swarm. "We will leave this planet," says the Queen. "It is far too dangerous, even for its brave and noble inhabitants. Thank you friend," she says to you. Then she and the lieutenant scurry off.

A few moments later, lights flash up into the darkening sky. The Skree are gone forever.

THE END

from page 53

You put on your most innocent face. "Here's what happened, sheriff," you say. "I was hiking through the woods when I heard loud yelling behind me. Next thing I knew, all these guys were chasing me."

You shake your head. "Would *you* have stopped to ask what was going on? One of those guys had a *gun*. So I got out of there as fast as I could."

"What about this creature that they saw?" the sheriff asks.

"Creature? I didn't see any creature. All I saw was a bunch of people yelling."

The sheriff shrugs his shoulders. "Summer craziness. Well, you're all free to go."

Robbins stays to argue with the sheriff, which turns out to be lucky for you. When you step out of the office, you see a glowing shape rise from the park. It hovers for a moment, then streaks for the horizon.

You smile. If Mr. Robbins had seen that, he probably would have had a fit.

THE END

102

The entire hill is honeycombed with tunnels and passages. "Wow!" you think. "These guys have done a lot of work." Your only answer is a harder shove from your guard's jaws.

As you go deeper, a glowing slime on the tunnel wall lights your path. The musky smell grows stronger. Finally, you're pushed into a huge underground chamber. Hundreds of Skree-creatures stand about, nodding and bowing, or marching back and forth to the center of the room.

"Yuck!" you gasp. When you see what's in the center of the room, you're afraid you're going to get sick. It's a creature with a tiny Skree body. Its head, however, is a huge pulsing mass. It wobbles back and forth as other creatures report to it.

Welcome, Earthling. A voice seems to echo inside your skull. *I am the Brain. All these others are my arms and legs. You will tell me about your planet.*

You've had enough of being pushed around. But what should you do?

Should you attack this horrible thing? Turn to page 62.

Should you try to find out what it wants? Turn to page 109.

from page 99

You follow the flying robot back to what looks like a construction site, right into a huge black dome.

The whole dome is filled with computer gear. As you stop to catch your breath, the dome entrance crashes shut behind you. "An organic life form," a deep voice rumbles from huge speakers. "I have not seen your like in a long, long time."

"Who are you? *Where* are you?" you shout.

"I am the Supreme Intelligence," the voice goes on. "I am this entire dome."

"A-a computer?" you say.

"The best ever created. I was built in a distant galaxy by organic life forms much like you. They were losing a war. So they built me and the robots you've seen."

"Why?"

"For revenge. My basic programming is simple. Kill all organic life forms wherever I find them. Since then, my robots and I have wandered the universe, performing my sole function."

"How long has this been going on?" you ask.

"For the last 73,000 of your years," replies the Supreme Intelligence. "And every population I've discovered, I have exterminated."

Turn to page 67.

104

As you run, you stare over your shoulder. The occupant of the wrecked car comes staggering out —a headless robot. You head for a nearby forest. It looks like you'll make your escape. But from behind the trees come more robots. You're cut off!

A huge, rusty robot reaches for you with its metallic hand. From its speakers come the words, "Supreme Intelligence demands . . . death to all organic life . . ." The hand clamps on your arm as other robots surround you.

Although you know it's hopeless to resist, you try to pull free anyway. Amazingly, you succeed! The robot's rusty arm snaps off.

Flying across the circle of robots, the metal arm smacks into another automaton's head. Metal plates rain to the ground as the second robot falls to pieces.

Turn to page 99.

106

from page 98

You freeze as the shaggy alien stares in your direction. Then the alien's ears twitch again as it turns its head away. Apparently, it didn't see you.

Suddenly, you hear a rustle behind you. Whirling around, you see a shaggy alien pointing a glowing power-rod at you. HISSSS! Darkness overcomes you.

Turn to page 15.

You turn to make a run for the boat, only to discover another Skree-creature has appeared behind you. Unfortunately, this one not only has claws but also a huge stinger. It's also about twelve feet tall. You have nowhere to turn.

The creature advances on you until its huge jaws touch your chest. Then it starts pushing you.

"Want me to go somewhere, huh? Right, sure." You realize you're babbling, but you can't stop. The huge Skree marches you away from the shore and up a hill. "Nice day for a walk, isn't it? Heh-heh. HELP!" you scream.

No help arrives. Instead, the Skree nudges you into a tunnel leading underground. It reminds you of a giant anthill.

The place smells of damp earth and a peculiar musky odor, an odor you've noticed from your Skree guard. You start descending into the hill.

If you decide to make a run for it in the tunnels, turn to page 88.

If you let your guard lead you where you're supposed to go, turn to page 102.

from page 32

"I'll go with you," you say to Hool and the other aliens.

"You'll still need this," one of the humans says, handing you a foot-long rod. "It's both a tool and a weapon." You get a quick demonstration of the rod's three settings: The first lifts objects off the ground. The second stuns animals and people. The third setting is ZAP, which vaporizes anything.

Hool and the other aliens are eager to go. Soon you're deep in the forest, doing your best to keep up.

The Arfa are marvelous trackers. Hool finds footprints and broken twigs that mark Samuels' trail. Sometimes he stands still, sniffing the air for some trace of Samuels' scent.

Now you hear noises ahead of you. It sounds like somebody running wildly through the forest. The thief!

Finally, you catch a glimpse of a running man in a dark jacket. He has one of the glowing rods in his hand. Instantly, Hool raises his rod and fires.

The rod is obviously set on ZAP. Although the ray misses Samuels, it slices through a tree trunk behind him. The tree crashes to the ground, pinning Fred Samuels.

Turn to page 85.

"Since you went to all this trouble getting me here, I suppose I should listen," you say.

Foolish Earthling! I detect this strange thing your life form calls humor. It will do you no good. Not against the Swarm of Skree! The sheer power of the thoughts silences you.

The greatness of the Swarm is beyond your puny comprehension. We have destroyed and eaten all other Swarms. Our Swarm completely covers our Home World. But now the Skree are dying, for there is no room left on the Home World.

It takes a little getting used to: a race that eats its rivals. But the Brain goes on. *Other worlds have much room—like this one. So the Swarm of Skree has come to this planet you call Earth. It will make a fine new Home World, after we eliminate the Soft-skins called humanity.*

This announcement makes you wonder exactly what your part in the Brain's plans may be. It's almost as if the creature reads your mind.

But for the time being, I will need advice on these humans. You can stay and serve me, or join the other prisoners in the Pit.

If you accept the Brain's offer, turn to page 76.

If you join the prisoners, turn to page 52.

Fred Samuels tells everything he knows about the Arfa to the interested rangers. When he finally finishes his story, a ranger turns to you. "What can you tell us about this?"

You think fast. "It's just the way he said. But the aliens weren't big and shaggy. They were little green men."

Fosca picks it up. "No, they weren't. They were the Purple People from the Planet Garbalon. They gave me the secrets of anti-gravity. I've got them here somewhere . . ." He starts looking through his knapsack.

"That's enough!" the ranger says. He and his partners start leaving the watchtower. "Flying-saucer nuts," he mutters, walking away.

"Hey! Hey, wait!" Samuels says.

Fosca just grins and winks at you. Your secret is safe.

THE END

Right now, all you want is O-U-T! You dash for the door, followed by the alien who warned you. She pushes you across the hall, into another doorway. When the other scientists appear, she points down the hall. The shaggy scientists all take off on the false trail.

Your secret friend walks to your doorway, removing an object from the pocket of her smock. It's a disk about the size of a quarter which she presses to your forehead. It sticks.

She does the same thing with another disk to her head. "I hope you understand me, because we don't have much time. I'm Eeyipp, of the Gu'ur. My people are looking for new Home Worlds. They intend to conquer your planet.

"Not all the Gu'ur support this aggressive policy. That's why I'm setting you free to warn your people. If our scouts find your planet well-prepared, they'll call off the attack."

Eeyipp hands you her power-rod, showing you its settings and how much power it fires. "Bring this weapon as proof.

"I'll show how you can get out of this building," she adds. "But I can't help you once you're outside..."

Should you head for your boat? Turn to page 59.

Should you head for the hills above the camp? Turn to page 35.

from page 54

"If the Skree have this sickness, all I need is a hiding place," you tell yourself. "Then I can let the disease take its course."

Yet finding a hiding place in an over-sized anthill isn't easy. How do you know which tunnels are heavily traveled and which aren't?

As you search for a safe place, you find several more plague victims. They all run away from you. "You'd almost think *they* were trying to hide!" you think. Some tunnels are littered with bodies.

At last, you come to a heavy, grated door closing off a tunnel. You think for a second. This is the first door you've seen since you entered the tunnels. It even has a guard—a warrior Skree lying on its side, claimed by the rust-plague. Whatever is on the other side must be important.

You creep up to the grating for a look. All you see are sick Skree, milling around a large room. So this is why the sick Skree were hiding. This is a plague-prison! The healthy Skree are locking up the sick ones.

"Not for long, though," you say to yourself, unlocking the bolts on the door.

Turn to page 90.

114

"Well, I don't know," you say, emptying your pockets.

"Keys, penknife, pieces of string. What is this stuff? Old candy? Yuck! Wallet, money. Nothing useful," he says, handing back the stuff. "Is that all?"

"I guess so," you say. "Wait! How could I have forgotten this?" From your jacket you pull out a transistor radio.

"Are those batteries good? They're just what we need!" Conklin says. "We have everything but a power source for the timer. A couple of connections, and we'll be all set."

The prisoners form a human pyramid for one man to escape from the Pit. He carries a rope made from jackets torn in strips. Soon everyone is climbing out. Luckily, the Swarm didn't leave any guards. Conklin gives the orders.

"Prof, you, Vic, and Speedy set the bomb—as far down the lake tunnel as possible." Conklin turns to the group. "The rest of us scatter."

He grabs your arm. "If you'd rather, you can stick with me."

The bomb goes off with a deafening roar.

Should you take off on your own? Turn to page 86.

Should you stay with Conklin? Turn to page 40.

The Meson Communicator hums to life, sending your message out into space over and over again.

You rummage through a tool kit for something you can use to defend yourself. You finally choose something your Vorn memories call a *borpiz*-wrench. It has a solid feel in your hand as you stand guard by the door.

The wrench might not do much to stop the Vorn. But it may give these Falabb characters an extra minute to get a fix on your location. Although you've never met the Falabb, you're hoping they'll rush here to get revenge on the Vorn. They're the only chance you have to save the Earth.

The wait feels like forever. Suddenly, the whole ship is a bedlam of hooting alarms. A screen comes to life in the room. It shows a fleet of arrowlike ships flashing in. The Falabb have arrived!

Now you hear noise in the corridor outside. The Vorn are rushing to this room to take their battle stations.

Should you get out of the room before the Vorn get you? Turn to page 29.

Should you stay to direct the Falabb to this ship? Turn to page 58.

from page 68

Being up in the tree gives you a good chance to scout the ground below. "At least I lost that monster," you tell youself.

Then you realize something is moving down below. It's another Skree-creature. But this one is white, and smaller than the first one you saw. It's only four feet tall. But it has a much larger head than the first creature. Also, it doesn't have those menacing claws.

You suspect this is what the other creature was searching for. But as you lean forward for a better look, the branch cracks beneath you.

The Skree below turns. Its jeweled eyes see you. Then the creature scuttles away.

Should you follow the small Skree? Turn to page 25.

Should you get away while you still can? Turn to page 6.